STRONG WOLF OVERCOMES THE FLYING HEAD

Message from the Author:

Throughout my childhood attending Oneida Tribal School in Oneida, WI. Maria Hinton, one of our language teachers taught us the greatest rule in life; Honor the Creator, Honor Mother Earth and Honor Ourselves. As one of Oneidas Greatest Storytellers she opened a scientific world of the connection to the forest and our sacred connection in talking to animals and how they laid their lives down for us. This brought an overwhelming love for Mother Earth and a respect for myself, "that when the winds cry my name, what will be said about my life." Maria expounded on the legend of how powerful the forest is and that it is a witness of who we are as a people.

Long Ago there was a Legend of "Strong Wolf." It comes from the Iroquois people, who consist of Six Nations: the Oneida, Seneca, Mohawk, Onondaga, Cayuga and the Tuscarorans. Their traditional land is mostly in the state of New York. They are the only Native American People who consist of six nations. They were formed into a confederacy started from the Great Law of Peace, which came from the Peacemaker. In the Oneida Nation, an Oneida Grandmother was making a corn harvest meal, corn soup and corn bread, when she noticed through the window her grandchildren playing outside. She heard her grandson and granddaughter arguing. She watched and listened to their negative behavior and the negative words in how they spoke to each other, arguing back and forth and name calling. They started to push each other. "This has gone far enough with that behavior," she thought to herself.

She went to the door and called them in, "Charles and Sarah, come in for lunch." The children immediately stopped fighting, shocked that they were busted, for they did not know anyone was watching or listening to them.

As they came inside the house, the Grandmother gently washed their hands with a damp cloth and kissed them on the head. The kitchen smelled so good with the corn bread and corn soup. The brother and sister sat down at the table.

The Grandmother served them two big bowls of corn soup. Next to it she placed a slice of corn bread on a small plate with a little bit of butter. "Ok, as you two eat your lunch, I'm going to tell you a story." Embraced in their Grandmother's love, they listened attentively.

"Many winters ago, near Oneida Lake, there was an Oneida settlement. In this village there were people whose hearts had become lazy, and they forgot the sacrifice of their protection and of the Great Peace. They were always quarrelsome. Arguing with everyone, they began to hate their own blood. It became such a great problem, that a gathering was called out to all the people.

A powerful Chief among the Oneidas stood up and began to talk to the people. "There is a Great Darkness among our people. I walk through our village and I hear negative words and negative actions in behavior to each other. It is bringing fear and doubt to our people. This Black Matter of negativity is causing a hatred for our own blood! It must stop! This is a Warning, that if we don't embrace Peace, Power and Righteousness under the Great Law of Peace and live for each other in joy and happiness, who knows what this Black Matter will become?

"I plead with you to embrace the victory of our struggle in preserving our bloodline as a people. Represent us with kindness and love, Mother Earth is watching. The trees and animals are witnesses to who we are as a people. They watch and listen to us; this is how they know us. Mother Earth is a strong force, if we do not behave ourselves and represent her in harmony and peace, who knows what she will release."

Everyone listened to the powerful chief and what he had to say. Among the people there was a boy who embraced the warning in his heart. His name was Strong Wolf. Strong Wolf wanted to help protect the people, so he placed his bark house at the edge of the village. This way he could keep a look out and warn the people of what was coming to the village.

There were two large wolf-like dogs who followed him, for they loved to be by him; they never left his side. Such a bond of oneness immersed between Strong Wolf and his two dogs. Their thinking was so connected that when Strong Wolf hunted, the dogs would circle around and drive the game towards him, working in oneness. Every hunting trip was bountiful. The extra meat he would give to the widows and orphans to show his love for the people.

Strong Wolf was so admired by his thoughtful behavior in living for others, always helping those in need. Whenever they sought to pay him for his good deed, Strong Wolf would be skipping away, "It's all good, no need," and he'd be walking away with a wave and a smile. Because of the intent of his heart was so great he was blessed with great speed.

Despite his young age, he was very wise, so much that the Council would choose him to pass important messages from one chief to another, for his opinion was greatly respected. When a very important message had to be posted from one chief to another chief, the elders would always ask for Strong Wolf, as he was greatly trusted, attentive, a good listener, and wise.

Strong Wolf was not only wise, but he was blessed with great strength. He would take great flight in a lacrosse game. Connecting with the wind and creation all around him, he would play in a peace of mind, so that the ball would always go where he placed it. To watch him play was like watching a thunderstorm embrace the sky.

He would use the same mindset to prepare for a long hunt. But this time it was different. He felt strange. He noticed different patterns in the clouds.

"How strange," he thought to himself.

As he was pressing forward, he walked under a tree and become tangled up within its branches as if it was trying to hold him back, "I must get food for the people," he thought and pressed forward.

As he crossed a little opening in the river a sudden huge wave grabbed him. "How funny, as if it was trying to hold me back."

"I must get food for the people," he repeated and pressed forward. Soon they were moving West, down the trail. The dogs felt uneasy at Strong Wolfs' apprehension, they knew something was wrong. They nodded to each other and went into protective mood. One dog walked out front of him, to protect his mind and one dog walked behind him to protect his heart. They carefully proceeded.

Throughout the day, they noticed the silence of the forest. No signs of any birds except for the hummingbird, who kept bringing his presence of alertness in flying right in front of Strong Wolf's face.

Strong Wolf said, "How strange! It was as if she was trying to whisper a message." Still they continued. They kept seeing bunnies diving into their burrows. For two seconds they were there and then they were gone. The squirrels kept chucking acorns at them. One hit Strong Wolf on the head and the dog barked at the squirrel to stop it. So the squirrel did, dashing and disappearing up the tree.

"What is this matter, why is the darkness silencing the forest?" thought Strong Wolf. He looked for any rubbings of deer or the scent of any bears, but nothing. He noticed the closeness of his two dogs, that their hair on their backs rose, and their tails were behind them in fear. Something grabbed their attention to the north and confused them with its scent. They growled knowing that something subhuman was infecting the forest. "What has the forest released?" Strong Wolf knew he had to reevaluate the situation.

So they made camp and lit a fire. "Let us pray and give thanks and ask for protection in offering food up to the Creator. Let us eat to calm our hearts and give strength to our minds, so we can remove any negative thoughts and focus on pure thoughts. For whatever is coming to attack us, we must have a clear mind." Strong Wolf began to cook the meat with such warmth and he began to feed the dogs with great care. As he fed them he petted them on the head, "It will be okay." With a smile on his face, he feed the dogs.

One of the dogs looked up to him and began to speak, "You are a true friend," the dog said to him. Strong Wolf startled with shock and stared at him. "Do not be surprised, for we could always speak to you. Most human ears are closed, because their hearts are closed, but I know you listen with your heart. The Negativity of the village has made Mother Earth release a Black Matter Spirit, a monster. It has been released to destroy the village. You must run back and warn them.

"Only then, the protection of forgiving each other will stop the monster from destroying the village. They must pray to change to embrace the good. Only forgiveness can stop this monster. Go...Run to the village and warn them. I lay my life down for you for I know you are a respecter of life. A black matter monster who feeds off fear and doubt is heading right for our camp. Run with might to the village and warn them." There was hope in the dog's eyes, so proud, for he believed in Strong Wolf.

Immediately, without hesitation, Strong Wolf threw his personal belongings to the side and said, "Great Father, forgive me of my weakness, that I may do better. Please grant me the speed to reach the people to warn them to correct our behavior." As he began to run down the trail, Strong Wolf heard the past chiefs cheering his name. "You can do it, Strong Wolf…You can do it, Strong Wolf!" he heard them cheering. Just then he felt the spirit of the trees release their energy to him and a bolt of speed was given to him, for the trees are very forgiving.

For they knew Strong Wolf heart was
legitimate in changing his heart.   He could
hear the black matter monster coming up
right behind him and he leaped into speed.

Still the black matter monster of negativity charged towards them. Strong Wolf heard it screaming and it brought a shiver down his spine.

In curiosity, Strong Wolf turned to look at what was chasing him. To his shock, he felt a burst of rage. It was the Flying Head, and angry eyes glowed in his face, gnarled from negativity. The constant rage caused severe wrinkles to deform its face.

The violent screaming caused its teeth to become fangs and from the chaos of cruelty his hair could capture victims as if they were arms reaching out to grab you, to hold you back. It had no body, for it was subhuman, the only limbs were two scale-covered paws, with long curling claws that were used to destroy. It was truly a destroyer, sent to destroy, feeding off doubt and fear, a remedy for removing negativity. For negativity equals failure. Failure brings a cold heart, and it is failure that prevents you from moving forward in positivity.

Down the trail they ran. Leaping over sticks and bushes, fast and faster they ran, hearing it heavily breathing right behind them. They dove into an old badger hole that went into the hill and came out the other side. The Flying Head was so big that it could not fit into the little burrow hole and it had to go around. Strong Wolf and his dog went out the other side and ran down the hill to the lake.

The dog said, "We tricked him, but it will not stop him. I will stay here, fight him, and lay my life down for you. Thank you for being a respecter of life; it is a great honor to have known you and to have been treated with such respect. I will never see you again on this earth. Farewell, good friend. May the Creator of all things protect you and give you the strength to protect the people." Strong Wolf greatly accepted his sacrifice from him, protecting Strong Wolf's life. He ran with hope, hope in reaching the village in time to warn his people.

As he ran, the clouds began to darken. He heard the thunder shake across the sky. Strong Wolf heard growls of great might in his dog's last great fight. In taking on this subhuman monster of Black Matter, he heard the dog's sounds of friction in dodging the great blows of battle. A final yelp of surrender, he knew his dog had been defeated. As tears filled his eyes, Strong Wolf ran fast and faster, telling himself that he was going to make it.

Coming into the home stretch, he felt a great burst of hot air. Strong Wolf turned and saw the monster regenerating its speed by absorbing the power of the trees it magnetically drew from the root to the top of the trees. Over and over, it hurtled each tree, so quickly, with nothing standing in its way. It was almost caught up to Strong Wolf.

Strong Wolf began to pray for his people. "Oh Creator, forgive my people. I pray that we will have peace in our hearts. I pray that we may appreciate each other in being born on this earth. I pray that we will be satisfied with what we have been blessed. I pray that we may fight for every breath of life in renewing each day." With each prayer, he became fast and faster. In coming to a cliff, Strong Wolf dove off into a lake, confusing the Flying Head.

The turtle and fish grabbed him and sailed him across the lake, for all the creation understood the battle taking place to fight negativity affects everyone. As he reached the other side, they brought him the time he needed to prepare the people.

As he ran into the village, he was greeted by the chief, "As I was resting, I dreamed a horrible monster was attacking you and was told to organize the people and wait at this entrance of the village. I was told that you have a message that would defeat this great monster and protect us from this evil. What is the message? What is the message?"

In all desperation he pleaded with Strong Wolf.

Strong Wolf looked at all the People confident eyes. He took a long breath to regain his stamina, and replied, "The message is Forgiveness...We must forgive each other and pray in unison BREATH IS LIFE, LIFE IS FORGIVENESS, POWER IS ONENESS." Immediately they turned and embraced each other with tears of renewing life. With arms held out, they all prayed in unison.

Just then a flaming burst of light of fire came over the hill. Hair, flying out in rage with glowing eyes, looking down on them. It released a large scream that shook the entire forest.

His fangs of fury made them cringe back. It claws reached out to grab them. They started to pray. All of sudden, a magnetic force from the trees pulled the Flying Head back, and back into the forest. Back to whence it came. The people fell to the earth crying, for they knew that there prayers were accepted. An enormous exchange of brotherly love renewed the people.

A Peace in their hearts towards each other was embedded. From that day forward, Strong Wolf was always watching and reminding the people of what Mother Earth can release. He was their witness to bring blessings to be blessed, for Mother Earth is always watching us and who or what it can release...

As the Grandmother finished telling the Legend, her grandchildren's eyes were big and filled with excitement, hanging on every word of the Legend. In taking a breath, her grandson looked up and said, "Grandma, thank you so much for sharing such a great legend of our people. I'm sorry for my behavior. I will work on doing better." He leaped into her arms and hugged her. The granddaughter also stood up, "Grandma, I, too, would like to thank you for reminding me on how to represent our people. I will do better." She also went closer to hug and kiss her Grandmother on the cheek. The Grandmother looked at her beautiful grandchildren, feeling so blessed and proud, grateful to pass on the great legend of how, "Strong Wolf Overcomes the Flying Head."

Burdeena Crosseta Endhunter © 2019

Special Thanks to: Calaway James Christjohn

Published by Phia Studios © Teelia Pelletier

ISBN-13: 978-0-9988513-4-1